SCREAMS IN SPACE

Raintree is an imprint of Capstone Global Library Limited, a company incorporated in England and Wales having its registered office at 264 Banbury Road, Oxford, OX2 7DY – Registered company number: 6695582

www.raintree.co.uk
myorders@raintree.co.uk

ISBN 978 1 4747 7202 0
23 22 21 20 19
10 9 8 7 6 5 4 3 2 1

British Library Cataloguing in Publication Data
A full catalogue record for this book is available from the British Library.

SCREAMS in SPACE

A HOLE IN THE DOME

BY STEVE BREZENOFF
ILLUSTRATED BY JUAN CALLE

raintree 🍃

a Capstone company — publishers for children

INTO THE DARK...

When you look up at the night sky, do you ever wonder if scary, creepy, horrible things happen up there just as they do on Earth? Sounds can't travel through outer space because there's no air. So if frightened people were out there, we'd never even hear their screams . . .

In *A Hole in the Dome*, humans live on a distant moon. A special dome protects them from their world's poisonous air. Nothing can live outside the space colony. But one summer, a girl and her brother spot a shadowy figure beyond the dome. What scares the girl most is that the figure doesn't look like an alien creature. It looks human.

Three million light-years from Earth One was a blue gas giant called Bastion. The planet had fifteen moons. Some were quite close to the large planet, and some were far away. One orbited in the middle zone: a red, dusty moon known to the people who lived on it as Rodmark.

No one, it was said, could survive on Rodmark – except within the moon's one huge city. The people there were protected by a massive dome of "hard light". The not-quite-clear energy surrounded the city and stopped anything getting in or out.

The domed city was called Lysande, from an old Earth One word that meant "shining". People liked to say their home was "a shining beacon in the dark and terrifying wilderness".

For that was what lay beyond the dome walls of Lysande. The rest of Rodmark was a horrible wasteland. Even the air was poisonous.

Only the toughest animals and plants lived outside of Lysande. There were stinging insects as big as dogs, with poisons that could paralyse. Plants grew leaves as hard and as sharp as steel.

Then there were the monsters. Each one was as tall as three grown men, and as wide too. It was said they moved so quickly that one could catch you, kill you and eat you before you even knew it was there. You'd barely have enough time to scream.

But stories like that were never true, of course.

Inside the domed city of Lysande, everything grew. Or at least, everything the Lysandians wanted to grow. Elm trees, maples, ferns and glorious green grass covered the land.

People of all races and beliefs made their home there too. All their ancestors had come from Earth One, hundreds of years ago. Although few people remembered that any more.

The centre of Lysande was busy, with skyscrapers that nearly tickled the top of the dome. Around the city, small neighbourhoods dotted the landscape. Each had winding streets or perfect grids. Each was also filled with friendly people who were outgoing and kind, or knew when to leave their neighbours alone and respect others' privacy.

That was the sort of place Lysande was. It had something for everyone, and each of its residents was happy.

A city completely inside a dome needed factories too, and farms. One such farm sat on the east side of the dome. It was so close to the thick, see-through wall that you could practically reach right out and touch it. And at the start of one summer Florence Harrison, better known to her family as Flossy, did just that.

"Don't tell Dad, OK?" Flossy said to her little brother, Benji.

If you asked her, thirteen-year-old Flossy was old enough to play by the stream. But if you asked Dad, she would never be old enough, especially with six-year-old Benji in tow.

"I know, I know," Benji said. He'd heard warnings like this from his big sister before. Benji loved the stream, even though it wasn't a natural stream. None of Lysande was natural. Everything had been built by the settlers.

The stream had no fish, no plants, not even a bit of algae. But Benji loved it all the same. It ran along the dome wall for the entire width of the Harrison farm. It kept their land safe from toxic elements that hid in the soil on the other side.

That was what Dad said, anyway.

"You can see all the way to the bottom," Benji said. He was lying next to the edge of the stream.

"So?" Flossy said. "It's only like a metre deep."

"The pebbles are pretty," Benji added, not bothered by how deep the stream was.

"Yeah," Flossy admitted as she sat on the grass next to him. It was still warm from the daytime "sun". Although the temperature inside the dome was carefully controlled, it had been decided long ago that Lysande should have the same seasons and climate of Earth One. Specifically, the dome weather copied a tiny section known as Nebraska.

So the nights were often chilly and always dark. The mornings were usually cool and clear. The afternoons were frequently hot and dry, and occasionally stifling.

Flossy looked down through the crystal-clear water. At the bottom were all kinds of pebbles. They ranged in size from as small as sand to as big as her fist. They came in all colours, and most were smooth after decades of covering the stream bed.

"Which is your favourite?" Benji asked.

"Favourite what?" Flossy replied.

"Pebble," Benji said. "Obviously."

"Oh, how obvious," Flossy said. "I don't think I have a favourite pebble." It was silver, in fact.

"Mine is that one," Benji said. He pointed with a stubby finger. "Green is my favourite colour."

"I know," Flossy said. In truth, though, Benji's favourite colour changed as often as the weather. "The green ones are herbicide."

"What's *herdaside*?" Benji asked.

"Herbicide," Flossy corrected him. "It's a thing that kills plants."

"Why?" Benji asked.

"Because," Flossy said, rolling onto her stomach, "the plants outside the dome are poisonous."

"Mr Yucky," Benji said. Every child in Lysande learned about Mr Yucky's face as the symbol for poison.

"Mm-hmm," Flossy agreed. "Every different colour pebble in there has a different job."

Benji seemed to think it over. "What about the silver ones?"

"Those keep out bad germs," Flossy said. "I think." She had learned all this in bits and pieces over her thirteen years. Some info she had got from her mum and dad, some from teachers and some from the neighbourhood kids.

"What about red?" Benji asked.

"They kill invasive animal species," Flossy said.

"What's *invadive aminal peaches*?" Benji asked.

Flossy rolled onto her back and looked up at the dome. Its top was tinted pale blue with fluffy white clouds during the day. But it was nothing more than a video display. Now the image was starting to dim to reveal the true starry sky beyond.

"Do you know what's outside the dome, Benji?" Flossy asked.

"Mr Yucky," Benji said.

"Right," Flossy said. "But there are also animals that are so mean and so scary that we call them monsters."

"Oh," Benji said, his voice quiet and scared.

"If any monsters tried to get inside the dome, the water in the stream would kill them," Flossy explained. She dragged a finger across her throat.

"And that's why the settlers made the dome, right?" Benji said. "To keep the monsters out?"

"Kind of," Flossy said. "But mostly it's there because we need different air to breathe than Rodmark has naturally. The air in here is good for us. Out there, it's poison."

"Mr Yucky," Benji said again.

Flossy still felt full from her second helping of Mum's cheesy biscuits, but Benji's bedtime was in just a few minutes. She sat up and sighed.

Tomorrow was the last day of school before the summer break. Flossy's friends were looking forward to pool parties and camping. Some even had trips planned to an amusement park on Habasher 7, a nearby moon. They all lived in the middle ring of the dome. There everyone lived in a small house next to another small house on a pretty curved street with lots of trees and neighbours.

But Flossy lived on a farm in the outer ring. When school finished, she would be put to work. Summers on a farm were very busy.

"Oh, look!" Benji said. He was next to her on his back now too, looking up at the stars. "There's Bastion!"

The huge planet that their home orbited took up half the sky. They could only see it at night, when the video image of the blue sky faded and switched off.

"You know what that means," Flossy said. She sat up and stood. "Bedtime."

Benji jumped to his feet and said, "*Aww!*" But he was tired, and the walk back to the house was slow.

When they got home, Dad was asleep in his chair near the front window. Mum was on the sofa knitting. "Clean your teeth and get ready for bed, both of you," Mum said, "and don't disturb your father."

Flossy kneeled next to Benji's bed. Her little brother lay under his blanket. Although his eyes were still open, sleep had already begun to pull him away.

"I saw a boy outside the dome," Benji said, staring at the ceiling. "Just before we came inside."

"Oh yeah?" Flossy said. Ever since he began to talk, Benji had been making up imaginary friends, imaginary pets and even imaginary brothers and sisters. "What did he look like?"

"He was bigger than me," Benji said, "but smaller than you. He had hair like yours."

"You mean brown?" Flossy asked.

Benji shook his head. "I mean long," he said. "But all messy, like yours if you don't brush it."

"I always brush it," Flossy said.

"I know," Benji said. "His hair was orange and messy and long. And his face was dirty."

"Well, it would get dirty living outside the dome, I expect," Flossy said.

Benji looked at her. "Could someone live out there, really?" he asked.

"No," Flossy said. "Remember? Mr Yucky?"

"Maybe it's safe for the people who are already there," Benji said, staring at the ceiling again.

"Well, we'll never find out," Flossy said. She hoped that would put the matter to rest.

"We could go out there," Benji said. "You could probably make a hole in the dome so we could."

"Don't let Dad hear you say that," Flossy said. "He doesn't like us even getting close to the stream. Besides, it's illegal."

"It is?" Benji asked.

"Of course," Flossy said. "Tampering with the dome is a crime. I know a girl at school who got into big trouble just for scratching her name into an anchor." Anchors held the dome in place and created the hard light that made the dome's walls.

"What happened to her?" Benji asked.

"They moved her to a different school, I think. Far across Lysande," Flossy said. "I haven't talked to her since then. That was a long time ago."

The siblings were quiet for a moment. Then Flossy said, "You wouldn't want to have to leave the farm, would you?"

Benji didn't answer. He just rolled onto his side and closed his eyes. "Goodnight, Flossy," he said.

She kissed the top of his head and said, "Goodnight."

Flossy said goodbye to her closest friends. Both girls were leaving for a trip to Habasher 7 the next morning. Their families would enjoy beaches, skiing and roller coasters. Meanwhile Flossy would be busy cutting hay, weaning calves, and harvesting the first tomatoes and asparagus.

With Benji beside her, Flossy almost cried on the way home. The yellow hoverbus slipped out of the woody streets of the middle ring. It sped into the wide, open farmland of the outer ring.

Benji held Flossy's hand as they walked along Rural Route 3 after getting off the bus. Dad was at the front gate repairing the hinge. There was always something to fix on the farm.

"Florence," Dad said, using her real first name. That meant it was time to work. "The irrigation piping has sprung a leak somewhere along the secondary line."

"Where?" Flossy asked. She let her bag fall to the dusty ground next to the fence post.

Benji ran up the driveway towards the house. He was still young enough to enjoy the summer without any jobs to do.

"That's what you're going to find out," Dad said. He pulled off his work gloves. "The pressure on the south field is low. So start walking along the line between there and the main line till you find the leak."

Flossy sighed, rolled her eyes, and picked up her bag. She started walking towards the house.

"Florence," Dad said, leaning on the fence post.

She didn't answer.

"Florence, did you hear me?" Dad said.

"Yes!" Florence said without looking back at him. "I heard. I'll find the leak, OK? I just want to put my books away . . . and wash my face."

The south field was all soya beans and lettuces in alternating strips. At this point in the summer, that meant it was lots of green leaves.

The most beautiful, though, were the magenta flowers of the soya bean plants. They were very small and almost easy to miss among all the green, like purple freckles on a goblin.

The irrigation line brought clean water from the stream to the crops. Flossy's great-grandfather had laid it under the ground when he first started the farm.

The line's path was marked with little yellow flags as it wound its way from the stream to the fields. Flossy started at the south field and followed the trail of flags towards the stream.

It was a hot day. The sky video above was pure blue. There wasn't even a dot of white to offer a break from the "sunshine".

Flossy imagined she was walking on the irrigation pipe itself. She stretched out her arms as if she was balancing on a beam. Bees buzzed among the wildflowers between the fields. Those stretches of land weren't used for farming but instead were left wild to make sure the farm stayed healthy.

The yellow flags were spaced ten metres apart. Every time Flossy left one and started towards the next, she expected to find a puddle. The hole in the underground irrigation line would create a big patch of wet soil above. But she didn't find one.

After half an hour, Flossy reached the last flag. It was just steps from where the main line met the south line, and it was only a few metres from the stream.

And there she found her puddle. Her work boots squished into the wet ground. She pulled out one foot with a *thwack*.

Flossy pulled her mobile from her hip. "Dad," she said into it. "Found the leak. Flag south-one."

"All right, Flossy," he said. "Turn it off at the main line junction and hurry back for dinner. You and I will fix that break first thing in the morning. We can't have the whole south field going dry."

Flossy put away her mobile and started walking through the mud to the main line junction. There, she found the red spigot and turned it to the right until it stopped. The sound of water moving beneath her feet squeaked and then went quiet.

Flossy looked out towards the stream and the dome wall. Beyond that, she could see the rest of Rodmark. The poisonous part.

Lazily, she walked towards the stream and stood at its edge. The stream was only a few metres across, but she'd never gone through it. Dad had warned Benji and her about messing with the stream. He told them how important it was not only to the Harrison farm, but to all of Lysande.

Even germs on a pair of shoes could throw off the balance of the stream. Suddenly all the wrong algae would survive, or all the right plants would die or some fish monster would swim up from the gravel bottom and gobble up all the livestock.

Flossy would never dream of stepping into it.

But this afternoon, she did imagine that. She imagined taking off her wet boots and socks, rolling up the bottoms of her jeans and stepping right into the stream.

Flossy stared through the clear dome wall into the emptiness beyond. It wasn't *truly* empty, of course. The other side was mostly flat rock, and far in the distance were jagged mountains. Outside the dome, Rodmark was dusty. The wind seemed to swirl endlessly.

She just stared at it – forgetting all about the broken irrigation line, the dinner she was supposed to hurry home for, everything. And then she thought she saw a figure.

Flossy leaned over the stream, just a little, and squinted into the red dusk of Rodmark. There *was* something there.

Or some*one.*

It walked like a human. The image might have been stretched by the curved shape of the dome, but it seemed very tall. It was bent over and wobbled slightly as it walked.

It was so unclear in the whirling dust. But the figure was definitely coming straight towards her and the dome.

Flossy's mind raced. Had she done something wrong? Had she messed up the stream somehow? But she had only imagined putting her foot in the water . . . or had she actually done it?

What if the stream was ruined, and this monster could now cross?

But the dome. Surely the dome would protect her. It was there to keep out all the bad things of Rodmark.

Flossy's heart pounded as she struggled to pull her mobile from her pocket. She fumbled, and it dropped onto the grass.

Flossy gasped, dropping to her knees. She grabbed the phone just before it bounced into the water.

She looked up. The figure had stopped. It was no more than a few metres from the dome wall.

"Florence!" a voice called out behind her, and she jumped and turned around.

It was Dad, walking towards her from the house.

"Dad, there's a—" Flossy started to say. But when she turned to point at the figure outside the dome, she realized: the figure *was* her father. Or rather, it was his reflection in the dome wall.

"What's the hold up?" Dad asked.

"Nothing," Flossy replied. Her cheeks got hot. She suddenly felt embarrassed, as if she'd been caught playing with an imaginary friend. "I've turned off the south line."

"Well come on then," Dad said. He put a heavy arm around her shoulders. "Dinner's ready."

"Why didn't you call on the mobile?" she asked as they walked together towards the house.

"I tried, but there was no service at your end," Dad replied. "You were too close to the dome, I imagine. The wall causes all kinds of interference."

"I suppose," Flossy said. "Dad? Has anyone *ever* lived outside the dome? Like, a hundred years ago?"

Dad shook his head the tiniest bit. "I suppose the people who made the dome must have," he said. "They probably wore spacesuits the whole time and slept in temporary shelters to protect them from the air. Why are you wondering about that?"

"No reason," Flossy said quickly. She laughed lightly and added, "You know Benji's imagination. He said he saw a boy outside the dome yesterday while we . . . never mind."

"While we what?" Dad asked. His voice was suddenly stern. "Were you two playing near the stream again?"

"Just for a minute," Flossy said. She regretted bringing it up. "We weren't even playing really. We were just sitting on the grass and talking."

"By the stream," Dad added.

"Yes," Flossy admitted.

"Now, your mum and I have *told* you," Dad said, "we don't want Benji *or* you hanging around the stream except when necessary. And for a boy Benji's age, it's never necessary. You know what could happen if—"

"I know," Flossy said, cutting him off. "I'm sorry."

She stomped ahead, turning quickly to glance at Dad. But more than that, she was looking back through the shimmering dome walls. She couldn't shake the feeling that the figure she saw there wasn't Dad's reflection – that something on the outside had really seen her.

3

Dinner that night was as quiet as a funeral.
As soon as she had washed up her plate, Flossy
took Benji's hand and escaped the house.

Benji joined her excitedly. It was the first
summer night. He wanted to see the fireflies
that would be flickering as soon as "dusk" fell.

Flossy would've preferred anything to sitting in
the front room with their parents. Dad would read
silently, but his disappointment in her behaviour
would come off him like solar radiation. Mum's lips
would tighten into thin lines while she knitted.

Outside, the air cooled as the "sun" went down. The sister and brother walked between rows of baby broccoli in the north field. They were careful not to step on any of the crop.

On the far side, still fifty metres from the stream, Flossy lay on the warm grass. She looked up at the dome. Benji sat next to her and picked at the clover flowers.

"Stop that," Flossy said gently. "The bees need those."

"Sorry, bees," Benji said, but he didn't stop picking the flowers.

Flossy didn't care much. She was thinking about the figure she'd seen outside the dome a couple of hours before. She knew it was just her father's reflection. It had to be. But a small part of her wished for it to be something else – something *exciting*.

She decided she'd make it exciting.

"I saw someone outside the dome before dinner," Flossy said. She kept her hands folded behind her head and stared up at the dome as the day's video sky faded away.

Benji's face lit up. "Really?" he said. "Was it the boy I saw yesterday?"

Flossy smiled. "No, this thing was very big," she said, sitting up and letting her imagination go. "And it walked like this."

Flossy hunched her shoulders and held out her hands with elbows bent awkwardly. She let her mouth hang open and moaned like a zombie.

Benji's eyes widened, and he swatted at her. "Stop!" he screeched. "Don't be a monster!"

"I'm not, I'm not," she said. "I was just joking around. It wasn't a monster."

"I bet it was that boy I saw!" Benji said. "He probably wants to be my friend. Let's find him."

Benji jumped to his feet.

"No," Flossy said. She was remembering how disappointed Dad had been when he'd learned she'd taken Benji to the stream. "We can play imagination from here."

"Flossy!" Benji said. He grabbed her wrists and struggled to pull her to her feet. "This isn't imagination! There's a boy out there who needs our help! We need to save him from all the poisonous air and monsters!"

Flossy rolled her eyes but kept smiling. She let herself be pulled towards the stream.

By the time they reached the water, Benji wasn't pulling her any more. They were just walking hand in hand. They stood together at the bank and looked out into dusty Rodmark.

It was dark out there. It always was. Even during the day, the curling clouds of poisonous dust blocked out the greenish light from Bastion, the gas giant that Rodmark orbited.

It was dark inside the dome now too. Above them, the starry sky – of *real* stars – sparkled. The night felt magical. Summer nights often did, and the first night of summer even more so.

"We should get back," Flossy said gently. She squeezed Benji's hand. "Mum will start to worry."

"I want to look first," Benji said.

Flossy waited a few moments. "There," she said. "You've looked. Now–"

"What's that?" Benji said, cutting her off. He pointed into the swirling red darkness.

"What's what?" Flossy said. "It's nothing. It's . . ."

Except it wasn't nothing. There were lights outside the dome. They weren't very bright. In fact, they were so dim that Flossy couldn't see them if she looked right at them.

But when she pulled her gaze a little to one side, they appeared in the corners of her eyes. Several specks of pale yellow light, flickering like sickly fireflies.

She remembered seeing her father's reflection.

Flossy started pulling her brother away from the stream. "Come on, Benji," she said. "They're just the reflections of lights in the house."

She turned around and saw the spots of yellow in the distance. Each was a window in their home. But there were so few. There was the kitchen light over the dining table, the reading lamp next to Dad's chair and Mum's floor lamp where she sat against the arm of the sofa to embroider.

Flossy looked back at the dome and the wasteland beyond it. The specks of light were brighter now, and larger. It was as if they were moving closer.

"Let's go home," she said, squeezing Benji's hand tightly. "Let's go now."

Benji nodded, and hand in hand they ran back to the house.

Flossy cut into her cold scrambled eggs with the side of her fork, but she didn't take a bite.

"Aren't you hungry?" her father asked. He stood and carried his plate to the sink.

Flossy shrugged. "Not really," she said.

"Well, you'll work up an appetite this morning," Dad said. "Plenty of work to do around here."

He rinsed his plate, wiped it with a tea towel and put it back in the cupboard. After he'd left, Mum slid into the chair beside Flossy.

"Do you feel OK?" Mum asked. She pressed the back of her hand to Flossy's forehead.

Flossy shrugged again.

"I know my girl," Mum said. "Something's bothering you."

"Maybe," Flossy admitted.

"Tell me," Mum said. She got up from the table and leaned against the worktop.

Flossy took a deep breath. "When was the dome built?" she asked.

"The dome?" Mum said. She turned around and busied herself at the sink. "Didn't we have the three thousandth birthday celebration . . . When was that? The year Benji was born?"

"Oh yeah," Flossy said. Of course she knew that. "Who built it?"

"Come on now, Florence," Mum said. She turned back to Flossy as she wiped her hands on a towel. She wore her fake smile, the one she used on their neighbour Megan Teasdale, who Mum didn't like but was always polite to. "Haven't you studied Colony History at school already?"

"Yeah," Flossy said. "But when was the last time people – I mean, *our* people – lived outside the dome?"

"Well, I suppose it would've been a little over three thousand and six years ago," Mum said. She flung the towel on the oven door handle with a snap, as if that was the end of the conversation and she was happy to be finished with it.

Flossy wanted to ask more, but she couldn't put her finger on the right question. She just knew something about the dome – and the world outside it – didn't feel right.

"You'd better get moving," Mum said. "Your father may be half blind to his daughter's moods, but he was right about how much work there is to do this morning."

"All right," Flossy said, getting up.

"Your plate, love," Mum said. "Tidy up a bit, hmm?"

"I know," Flossy said, even though she had in fact forgotten. Her mind was on things far more troubling than the dishes.

It was a long, hot morning of work. But it was mostly outdoors in the sunshine, and Dad was in a good mood. Digging up and repairing the leaking irrigation pipe took most of their time before lunch. After that there was hay to cut and bale, and calves to feed.

At the end of the first day of summer, Flossy was tired. The moment her head hit the pillow that night, her eyes closed tightly. She was asleep even before Benji on the other side of the room had settled down enough to stop his pre-sleep chattering.

Maybe her brother's words were still worming into her ears. Maybe he was babbling about the dome, or about the boy outside the dome or about the flickering lights they'd seen the night before. Whatever the reason, Flossy found herself in a dream at the edge of the stream.

She looked down into the water. The pebbles at the bottom glittered like stars, and she stepped into the stream.

The water was ice-cold as it rose to her middle. The pebbles under her bare feet were smooth, but she could feel them sparkling against her skin.

She crossed the stream in a few steps and pressed her face against the dome itself to see outside. From so close, she could see it all now.

Beyond the dome wall were thousands upon thousands of people. They were not monsters, but people like her and her family. They were young and old, small and large. And they were forced to live out there, outside of the dome in wild Rodmark. They carried flickering lights, like the ones she'd seen the other night.

They were all rushing towards the dome, towards Lysande and the farm. Towards Flossy.

She backed away, but the stream water felt thick. It was hard to move. She tried to scream, but no sound came from her mouth.

Instead she heard the screams of the mob running towards her. The sound was muted by the dome, but she could still hear their anger.

As they got closer, she saw that the people weren't quite as human as she'd thought. They were bent and sick looking. Their eyes bulged, and their mouths hung open and let out moans.

Many carried not just torches, but shovels, picks and steel rods. They charged at the round wall and raised their tools like weapons.

None of those things could break through the dome. Flossy remembered that much from school. The dome was nearly indestructible.

But she was wrong. When the mass of people reached the dome, they brought down their weapons on the glittering hard light.

THUNK! THUNK! THUNK!

Flossy stumbled backwards and landed on the grass at the stream's edge. She stood up to run, but the dome wall started to crack. Then it shattered.

The poisonous air from outside rushed in and the good air from inside rushed out, forming a terrible twister.

The wind tossed Flossy and knocked her over. It picked her up and threw her against the crowd of people. They screamed and wailed and grabbed for her.

She fell to the ground. The people closed in around her and reached down at her. They groaned as if in great pain. Their dirty faces were thin and dry. They were hungry, sick, tired and worn through to the bone.

Flossy covered her face with her arms and screamed.

5

Flossy woke short of breath. Her room was still dark. Opposite her, Benji was sleeping soundly. His blanket was in a jumble at his feet.

The clock on the living room wall showed a little after four, but Flossy didn't care. She had to go to the edge of the dome.

The dream had seemed so real that Flossy believed some part of it might be. Not the part about an angry mob smashing through the dome. She knew that was impossible.

But *something* about that dream was true. Deep down, she had the nagging feeling that something about Lysande wasn't right. That they were all in danger, or her family was. She would find the answer at the dome, on the far side of the stream.

Flossy's heart pounded as she crossed the fields. The hems of her pyjama bottoms got damp from dew. She kept her eyes on the dome and Rodmark beyond. Then she saw them again. The twinkling lights in the far, dusty distance.

Were they reflections in the dome wall of the stars shining above? Or maybe some early morning light had found its way through the swirling dust and glittered off bits of sand.

Or maybe the lights were something more.

At the edge of the stream, Flossy crouched and rolled up her damp pyjama bottoms.

She looked into the clear water at the colourful

pebbles on the floor of the stream. In the darkness, though, they lost all their colour. Rather than a rainbow, they seemed dull and grey. It made the stream seem less magical and more mysterious.

Flossy took a deep breath and carefully stepped into the ice-cold stream water. It reached well past her knees, and soon her pyjama bottoms were soaked.

She pushed through the freezing water. She tried to forget that the pebbles beneath her feet released chemicals.

Dad always said the chemicals were safe for people and for all the good plants. But over the last few days, Flossy had begun to doubt a lot about Lysande. Dad had been so short with her when it came to the stream. Mum seemed unwilling to even talk about the dome.

Was this something new in the way her parents spoke to her? Or had they always been like this when she'd asked questions about life in Lysande, but she'd been too young to notice?

The stream was shallow on the far side where it met the dome's anchors. The anchors were complex metal equipment that Flossy couldn't begin to understand. She just knew they helped form the dome wall. They hummed constantly and quietly.

Flossy raised one hand, letting it hover just above the dome wall. She'd never touched the hard light before. As far as she knew, no one had. It was forbidden.

But the dome stretched for many kilometres in each direction. It was a huge globe hanging over their whole world. Surely some other curious kid had broken this little rule.

The dome wall crackled. Tiny sparks bounced between her palm and the wall. It was as if the wall wanted to be touched.

Flossy put her hands on the hard light of the dome. It sizzled under her palms, but it wasn't painful. It was gentle, like the bubbles popping at the top of a glass of fizzy drink. It made her smile.

But as she gazed through the dome wall, all Flossy could see was the familiar red, dusty nothingness. No lights. No people.

She heard the wind, though – the wind outside the dome. It sounded wild and strong, as if a gust would knock her down.

Except it couldn't be the howl of Rodmark's winds. She knew the dome was soundproof.

The sound was not coming from outside, but from the ground near her feet.

Flossy crouched and found the source of the sound. Hidden by a fern and just beside one of the anchors was another device. It was a cube the size of a footstool. All the sides Flossy could see were solid black metal, except the side that faced into Lysande. That side was a slatted grate.

Flossy put her hand to the grate and felt the whoosh of warm air.

Air from outside the dome was coming into Lysande? But the Rodmark air was poisonous, wasn't it?

She pulled her hand away as if she'd burned it. She quickly pushed the fern's leaves back into place, trying to cover the vent.

Did I break something when I touched the wall? Or what if crossing the stream let in poisonous air? Flossy thought. But another part of her said, *That's impossible. The hole was already here.*

Flossy closed her eyes a moment and thought about Benji and her parents. She clenched her fists, got down onto her knees and took a deep breath at the grate.

The air smelled dry and slightly electric, like the clothes dryer just after Mum pulled out a load.

But Flossy didn't cough. She didn't turn green and fall to the ground to die. The air coming in was safe and not "Mr Yucky" at all.

Flossy trembled the whole way back to the house, her mind chilled and her pyjamas soaking. One thought stuck with her as she silently climbed back into bed: Mum and Dad, the teachers at school and everyone else were wrong about Rodmark – or they were lying.

6

Flossy ate breakfast quietly.

"You've been moody," Dad said as he poured coffee into his big, chipped mug. On one side, in faded pink, it read *Live the Life You'd Love . . . On Habasher 7*. Dad had bought it on the only holiday the Harrisons had ever taken. Flossy was only five, and Benji hadn't even been born yet.

"I'm just tired," Flossy said. "I had a bad dream last night."

"Oh yeah?" Dad said.

He sat at the table with his mug. Steam rose from the cup and twirled in the draft from the open window. It reminded Flossy of the swirling red dust of Rodmark.

"What was it about?" Dad said. "Not that old witch you used to have nightmares about, I hope."

Flossy smiled. She had forgotten about that nightmare. She hadn't had it in years. But when she was about Benji's age, it had terrified her.

An old woman, bent over with age or illness and wearing a dirty hood, would reach out a hand to Flossy. When Flossy backed away, the old woman would grab her wrist and shake her and laugh.

That was the whole dream, but Flossy had had it so often that for months she'd hated going to bed. She'd made her mum or dad sit holding her hands so the woman couldn't grab them.

"No, it wasn't that," Flossy said. She scooped up some beans and ate them one by one. "It was about the dome."

Dad ran a hand through his hair. "Aw, come on, Flossy," he said. "Is this going to become a thing?"

"No," she replied, but she went on. "I found this . . . this vent or something at the dome. It was letting in air from outside."

Dad laughed. "No it wasn't," he said. "Why would we want that air in here?"

Flossy shrugged.

"We wouldn't," he finished. "That's just an air circulator. They're all over, along with the anchors. They move the air, help the weather system, change the temperature, that sort of thing."

"Oh," Flossy said, somehow both relieved and disappointed.

Dad looked her straight in the eye. "I've heard about kids getting interested in the dome at your age. They want to know what's outside," he said. "Trust me, it's nothing you want to see firsthand."

"I know," Flossy said. But in fact, she *did* want to see the rest of Rodmark firsthand.

Dad took a long swig of his coffee. He sighed as he put down the cup.

"Take it from me, Florence," he said. His voice was softer now. "I've seen what can happen to kids who take too great an interest in that *dome*."

He said *dome* as if he hated the thing. It had never occurred to Flossy that anyone *could* hate it.

"Mum and I both grew up near the dome, just like you and Benji," he said. "We know almost everything about it. And between us, even stuff most people don't know and should never find out."

"What do you mean?" Flossy said.

Dad took a long moment of quiet. He watched the kitchen doorway. In the other room, Benji was on the carpet, pushing a toy lunar rover.

"Do you think I've never seen anyone outside the dome?" Dad said, almost whispering. "Do you think I'm blind?"

Flossy's heart seemed to stop. Her breath caught halfway to her lungs and she coughed. "Who–" she started to ask.

Dad cut her off. "Put it out of your mind," he said. He leaned across the table and took Flossy's hand. "Just do your work. Focus on what's happening right here, on the farm, in our community and in your school. The world outside isn't for us."

"But why–" Flossy said.

Dad stopped her with a hiss of air between his teeth. "I don't want you bringing this up again," he said. His anger bubbled until his face went red and his eyes seemed wet with tears. "Stay away. Stay on this side of the stream."

"Dad, *why?*" Flossy pleaded.

"If a Dome Maintenance patrol were to see you so close to the dome . . ." Dad trailed off.

"What would happen?" Flossy asked.

"You're putting yourself and the family in real danger," Dad said.

"How?" Flossy asked. "Why won't you explain it to me?"

Dad leaned back and started to open his mouth as if he might say more. But then he closed it and shook his head. "I can't," he said. "Just trust me. *Stay away.*"

"OK. I will," Flossy said. She felt her heart thump twice as if it had just remembered to begin beating again. "I promise."

Dad stood up. "I suppose you crossed the stream, then, if you found an air circulator."

Flossy nodded.

"I suppose Benji was with you," he added.

Flossy jumped to her feet. "He wasn't!" she said. "I swear, Dad. He was . . . he was in bed."

She could almost see the gears clicking in Dad's head. He knew Flossy had to have been out of bed after nightfall.

He let it go.

"Finish up in here," Dad said, "and get outside. Plenty of work to do."

For the next few days, Flossy managed to avoid the edge of the Harrison farm, the stream and the dome itself.

The dome was always there, of course. Its red glow washed over the outer fields, and the gentle crackle of hard light hummed constantly.

The dome filled Flossy's mind too. Especially the thought of what might be beyond it. But something in her dad's eyes the other day had scared her. So she kept herself and her brother as far away from the dome as possible.

It was a Thursday afternoon, just an hour or so before supper, when Mum noticed something at the kitchen sink.

"Flossy," Mum said.

Flossy was sat at the table with a book. It was one of Dad's old paperbacks. It told a spooky tale about a trip to Mars written long before there had really been any trips to Mars.

"Yeah, Mum?" she said. She wasn't quite listening, though. Her mind was on the story.

"The pressure seems low again," Mum said. She turned on the tap. The water came out in a slow, weak stream. "Would you mind running over to the main junction and seeing what's up?"

Her mind still half on Mars with the characters in the book, Flossy stammered, "Wh-what? Oh, sure. Yes, Mum." She put the book down and went to pull on her trainers.

Flossy was halfway across the fields when she realized what she'd agreed to. She was about to walk up to the stream. She'd be as close to the dome as she could get without crossing the water.

Her heart beat faster. She gripped the handle of her toolbox tighter and clenched her jaw.

"This isn't a big deal," she told herself as she reached the stream.

The junction where the water for the house broke off from the main line was marked above ground by an aluminium stump. It had a digital readout that showed the current water pressure. It was definitely low. But the ground below Flossy's feet was dry. That meant the leak was somewhere else.

Flossy looked around. Her eyes settled across the stream at the edge of the dome. She wasn't sure, but the ground there seemed soaked.

Flossy pulled the mobile from her hip. "Dad," she said into the phone.

It crackled back, but she didn't hear him.

"Dad or Mum, you there?" she tried again.

Still just static and dead air.

Flossy put her mobile back and took a deep breath. It had been very hot all day, and Flossy still wore shorts. She stepped out of her trainers, pulled off her socks and walked into the water.

She gasped at the freezing temperature. "How is it so cold after such a hot day?" she muttered.

She walked on, sometimes flinching when her foot found a rare sharp pebble. She climbed up to the other side.

Her bare foot sank into the wet ground up to her ankle. There *was* a puddle there, a deep one.

Flossy put her toolbox down and reached a hand into the muck. She felt warm water flowing against her palm.

Then the leak was close – really close. Flossy pushed her hand through the mud until she found the water line. She could feel a crack in the rubber seal. When she curled her fingers around it, the water stopped.

The seal would have to be replaced. Flossy pulled her hand out of the ground and searched through her toolbox. She found her spanner, a new rubber seal and a hand pump to drain the puddle.

She'd also have to switch off the water or fixing the leak would be impossible. She looked over her shoulder. The nearest shut-off for the community water was about fifty metres away, on the other side of the stream.

Flossy sighed and grabbed her wrench. But as she stood, she saw a fern beside an anchor. It was the same one that hid the vent, and it was right at her feet. Somehow, she hadn't noticed it before.

She looked towards the house. For a moment, she saw Dad. He was walking out of the barn. Then he was gone, inside the toolshed.

As she stood there by the vent, Flossy thought she could smell the air coming through. It was warm and dry and metallic.

Move the fern, her mind seemed to scream as she squeezed the spanner in her hands.

Flossy took a deep breath and turned to look out across Rodmark. Her face was so close to the dome now. She smelled the crackling electricity of hard light. The evening sky – in tones of pink and orange and violet and blue – still showed on the dome above her.

But at her level, the dome was clear. Flossy looked out into the swirling red.

She wasn't even surprised when she saw a figure out there, looking back at her.

Dad had all but told her they were there and that he'd known about them forever.

She stared at the figure opposite her. It seemed to stare back. Flossy wondered what it thought of the Lysandians inside the dome, where there was green grass, clean water, plenty to eat . . .

And happy families.

The figure looked like a boy, Flossy decided. He didn't seem much older than Benji. She could not see the boy's face, but she imagined it to be dirty and pale and sickly. Like the desperate crowd from her dream.

Then that was the big secret: that people as human as Flossy and Benji and their parents were forced to live outside the dome. They suffered outside the dome.

And that meant everything Flossy knew about the dome and Rodmark was a lie. There were probably no monsters at all, no poisonous air – just people who needed help.

Flossy's heart swelled. She *would* help them. She would do it no matter what Dad said and no matter who thought this was best kept secret.

Flossy dropped to her knees, slapped the fern to the side, and slipped her spanner around the first bolt on the vent. She'd go outside and help that boy. She'd help them all. She'd let everyone into Lysande, where they could be happy and healthy and well.

It was hot. Not hot like back inside the dome on a summer day, where it was always sort of sticky. This was hot like the gust of air from the oven as it roasted a chicken for dinner.

The wind was stronger than the little gust out of the oven, though. Flossy covered her face with her arms as sand swirled around her. The little bits of red scraped her bare legs and feet, and she felt stupid for having dared to leave the dome without shoes and long trousers.

The air that pushed against her smelled familiar. It was the same dry, electric smell from that vent. So Dad was wrong, or lying. The vents had nothing to do with Lysande's weather systems. As far as Flossy knew, all the dome's air came directly from wild Rodmark.

She could hardly see anything through the sandstorm. But between her squinting and her tangled fingers covering her eyes, she could just make out that figure. It was that little boy.

"Hello!" she called out, but her voice was lost in the roar of the storm.

The boy seemed to be running away from her, or running as much as someone could in this horrible wind. Flossy shouted again. This time her voice never left her mouth as the sharp pieces of sand and dust swirled into her throat and choked her.

Flossy pulled her T-shirt over her mouth and coughed. She couldn't see the boy at all now. She just stumbled along the rocky ground.

The sky flashed with pale red light. A moment later, thunder clapped over the howling wind. At first Flossy expected it to start raining. But something told her Rodmark didn't get much rain, if any.

"Hello!" she called again. She heard no answer.

Flossy pushed on blindly through the wind. Then her foot caught on something hard, and she fell to the ground.

"Ugh!" Flossy cried as sharp rocks dug into her already sore skin.

Flossy pushed herself up and sat on the dry ground. The sand kept flying around her, stinging like a thousand angry hornets.

But something else rushed past – something big. Its body brushed up against her T-shirt. Her hair stood straight up.

"Who's there?" Flossy yelled.

There was no answer except the screams of the wind. A moment later, something rushed past her again.

"Please!" Flossy shouted. "I just want to help you!"

Still no reply. But she could just barely hear something else through the wind. It was a low growl, like one of the Harrisons' barn dogs when the postman came.

Flossy struggled back up to her feet. *I have to go back to Lysande*, she thought suddenly. *This was a mistake.*

With her T-shirt over her mouth and one hand over her eyes, Flossy ran. She couldn't even see the glittering hard light of the dome in the thick clouds of red dust. She just picked a direction and hoped it was the right one.

She struggled forward. The sand stung against her legs and arms and cheeks. Her heart seemed to stop as she heard more growls and snarls behind her.

Flossy screamed and tripped through a heavy mound of sand, tumbling to the ground. She coughed violently into her hands and tasted copper.

She turned and opened her eyes despite the storm. The sand burned. Her eyes filled with tears as she looked around, sure she'd see a pack of monsters about to pounce.

But she saw only that boy.

He was close now and running towards her. His body was covered with dirty rags, and a beaten-up looking helmet protected his face. Only his eyes showed through.

The wind and sand blew even harder, and Flossy fell back into the dirt. The last thing she knew was the smell of red sand swarming into her nose and her mouth. It choked her until everything went black.

9

"She's waking up," a faraway voice said.

No, not faraway. It was muffled, but nearby.

Flossy heard the harsh wind of Rodmark.
It whistled as if sneaking through a crack.

"Give her some water," the voice said,
no longer muffled. It sounded like a woman.

Flossy's head was clearing. She opened her
eyes. It was dark, but she could see a little: eyes
looking down at her and old clothes that were
more like rumpled sheets and dirty rags.

"We don't have any," said a boy's voice.

The woman sighed. "Really, Aylin," she said. Her voice was sharp, like Dad's got sometimes. "We had a litre and a half."

"Poli finished it," Aylin replied.

"Sorry, girl," the woman said to Flossy. "You'll have a dry throat until Aylin can get back to the well."

"I'll go now," the boy said.

Flossy's eyes got used to the low light. She saw the boy hurry away. Then she looked up at the old woman crouched over her.

The woman's eyes were tired looking and red around the rims. Her pale skin was rough and worn. Flossy nearly reached up and touched it, wondering if it felt more like old leather or a crumpled paper bag.

"You're really here," Flossy whispered. "There are people living outside of Lysande. And you are worn to the bone."

The woman nodded slowly. "To the bone is right," she said. "Every last one of us."

"Are there many?" Flossy asked.

The woman shrugged. "Hundreds?" she said. "Thousands? Tens of thousands? I can't begin to guess."

Flossy was quiet, and then she remembered the boy, Aylin. He must have been the same person she'd called out to in the storm.

"The boy goes out there alone?" Flossy asked. "But he's so young."

"Aylin is almost ten," the woman said. "That's plenty grown-up if you live here."

"Oh," Flossy said. Something caught in her throat, and she coughed. She could taste copper again.

"The air out here takes some getting used to," the woman said. "Most of us faint like you did when we're in it for the first time."

She didn't say those words with any care or concern. She didn't gently push Flossy's hair back from her forehead, like Mum did when Flossy was sick with flu or had taken a hard fall off an unbroken horse. Instead the woman simply said them like they were facts – boring old facts.

"Where am I?" Flossy asked. She was feeling a few steps behind.

"I think," the woman said as she got up from her crouch and groaned, "what's more important is where you're not. And you're not in Lysande any more. You're outside the dome."

Flossy sat up with some difficulty. Her head spun and ached, but she could get a better look at the room now. It was more like a hovel.

"Do you . . . live here?" she asked.

"Yes," the woman said. Flossy watched as she sat in a chair nearby. "It's my home. And Aylin's and Poli's. She's about your age. You fourteen?"

"Thirteen," Flossy said. "I'm tall for my age."

The woman shrugged. "But they're not *my* children," she went on. "I let them stay here, though. They're useful to me."

Flossy wiped a hand across her cheek. Her skin was gritty with red sand. "Like, they work here?" she asked.

"Of course," the woman said. "Everyone out here works, all the time."

Flossy shook her head. "They should be allowed to be kids," she said. "It shouldn't matter if they're useful."

The woman laughed. But it didn't have any humour or joy.

"Anyway," Flossy said as she stood up, "I'm here to take Aylin and anyone else who wants to come back into Lysande."

The woman frowned. "Back into Lysande?" she repeated, her voice deep and quiet. "Child, what are you talking about?"

"The vent–" Flossy started.

But at that same moment, a door on rickety hinges swung open. It slammed into the outside wall of the shack. The sound of Rodmark's wind roared and howled into the room and drowned out Flossy's words.

Two people practically fell into the hovel. They were both covered head to toe in ragged clothes and old gear. Everything was stained red.

They pulled up their goggles. One of them was Aylin, the boy from earlier. The other must've been Poli.

"Some water," Poli said. She held out a metal container. Its only lid was a strip of cloth strapped on with an elastic band.

Flossy took it and watched as the kids removed their masks. Both of them looked unwell. Their cheekbones were sharp, and their hair was thin.

But it was Poli who caught Flossy's attention. The girl looked familiar. Her face was pale and scarred. Around her eyes, where the helmet didn't cover her face, the skin was grimy and dry.

Flossy felt guilty for taking the first sip of water, but she started to take the lid off.

"Drink through the fabric, child," the old woman told her. "It keeps out the grit."

"Oh," Flossy said. She looked at the dirty rag. It was the same clay-red as the sand. "I'm not really thirsty."

Poli took the container from her. "You'll get over that," she said. Then she took a long drink.

"I'm not getting over anything," Flossy said. "Because I'm going back to Lysande, and I'm taking anyone else who wants to come."

"Poli said things like that too," the old woman said, "when she first got here. That was years ago."

"But I really am," Flossy said. She turned to Aylin. "You found me, right? Near the dome?"

Aylin nodded. "You had fainted. I could tell from your clothes you'd just arrived. I thought Delilah would know what to do with you."

Flossy looked at the old woman. She must've been Delilah. Flossy nodded at her to say thanks.

"Can you take me back to that spot where you found me?" Flossy asked Aylin.

The boy shrugged. "I suppose," he said. "Better not try it until the storm calms a little."

"You should also put on some better clothes," Poli added. "The sand will tear your skin off in less than an hour if you go out like that."

Flossy ran her hands over her bare arms. Just the thought of cutting sand sent a shiver up and down her back.

"Fine," Flossy said. "But we should probably hurry. Someone might close the vent."

Poli found a set of heavy cloths. She tore them and tied the pieces around Flossy's waist, shoulders, face and head.

"Here," Delilah said. She handed Flossy a pair of bashed up old boots.

"Thank you," Flossy said. She pulled them on. They were a little too tight. "I'll give them back to you once we find the vent."

Delilah looked in her eyes. She didn't say anything, but Flossy could tell what the woman was thinking. *You'll never give them back, because you'll never get through that vent.*

10

It was a long walk back to the dome, and the violent weather of Rodmark made it even longer.

"This is the spot!" Aylin yelled. He had to shout to be heard over the wind.

Though the storm had died down, the wind still whipped up sand wildly. Flossy could hear and feel the tiny flecks scraping over her clothes, and she was thankful she had the extra protection.

She was more thankful, though, that soon she'd be back inside and away from here forever.

"I see the edge of the dome," Flossy called. She trudged towards it. The others followed close behind.

Soon Flossy spotted the big, black block of the anchor and vent, and she began to run. She folded one arm over her face and charged through the gritty wind.

Most of the anchor and vent were covered with red sand. Flossy dropped to her knees and began to dig through it.

But when she uncovered the vent, its grate was in place. Flossy tugged at it.

The metal cover wouldn't budge.

"This must be the wrong anchor," Flossy said, looking up at the others. "If my mum or dad had found it open, they wouldn't have closed it till they knew I was safe."

"I doubt your family closed it," Poli muttered. "It would have been Dome Maintenance."

Delilah shushed her.

"There are other anchors, only fifty metres in each direction," Aylin said. "We can check those."

Flossy stood up to go with Aylin, but Delilah held out a hand. "Wait. Look inside, child," she said. "Do you know this place?"

Flossy looked first at Delilah. The woman's tired eyes seemed as if they'd given up a lifetime ago. Then Flossy turned and looked into the dome, into Lysande.

It was difficult to see through the crackling hard light of the dome. And the "sun" inside was just starting to go down, covering Lysande in shadows. But there was a building in the far distance – maybe two.

"It could be my farm," Flossy said quietly.

"And them?" Delilah said. She put an arm around Flossy's shoulders and pointed towards the dome. "Look closer."

Flossy found who she meant. There were three figures in three sizes. It seemed to be a man, a woman and a child.

"That can't be my family," Flossy whispered. "They wouldn't just stand there."

"The boy seems upset," Aylin said.

And Flossy could see it now. The boy was trying to pull away, and the big one in the middle – the father – was holding him back.

For an instant, Flossy thought she could hear the boy scream her name, but it must have been the wind.

"It can't be them," Flossy said, backing away from the dome. She thought she might cry, but she held back the tears. "They're just . . . watching."

"I doubt they can see us through all the sand," Delilah said.

Flossy turned suddenly to Delilah, terrified. "How much of it is true?" she asked.

"How much of what?" Delilah said.

"The stories about . . . out here," Flossy said. "Is the air poisonous? Are the plants deadly? Was the dome made to keep Lysande safe? Are there monsters?"

Delilah put a hand on the dome. "It feels so cool and clean," she said. "Nothing like the rest of the world out here."

"Tell me!" Flossy shouted.

"The air," Delilah said, "is not poisonous. It is a little hard to breathe."

"And we can eat the plants," Aylin added. "There are some, if you know where to look. Some taste good too."

"And the dome?" Poli said, stepping up to Flossy. "They built that to keep *us* out."

"What do you mean?" Flossy said as she backed away from the girl. She was so familiar.

"Law-breakers," Poli said.

"Criminals?" Flossy said.

The girl nodded.

Aylin sat on his knees and pulled at the vent. He gave up quickly. "When I was eight, I pushed a girl off a climbing frame," he said. "I felt terrible about it. But I *was* violent, I suppose."

"That's it?" Flossy said.

"I scratched my name into one of the anchors," Poli said.

Something clicked in Flossy's head. Now she knew why the girl seemed so familiar. "You went to school with me!" Flossy said. "They said you'd moved . . . but that was ages ago. You were just a little kid!"

Poli kicked the ground. "An imperfect little kid, not fit for Lysande," she said.

Flossy turned to Delilah. "What about you?" she asked.

Delilah stared off. "I don't remember," she said. She chuckled. "Isn't that something? I don't even remember."

"Then the dome," Flossy said. "They only built it so . . . Lysande would be perfect?"

The others didn't answer. They didn't need to.

"But I'm not a criminal," Flossy said. Panic filled her voice. She looked from Poli to Delilah to Aylin. "I'm good to my parents and my little brother. I work hard at school and on the farm. I—"

The three stared at her.

"So there's been a mistake, right?" Flossy said. "I'm not supposed to be trapped out here. There has to be a way to let someone know!"

"You never broke the law?" Aylin asked.

"Of course not!" Flossy said. She spun to look into the dome. The three figures were closer now. They were just at the edge of the stream. *It couldn't be them.*

"How'd you get out here, then?" Delilah asked.

"I told you!" Flossy said. "I took off the vent and crawled out. It's not like I got arrested and thrown out here like you–"

"And isn't tampering with the dome against the law?" Delilah said.

Flossy opened her mouth to reply, but for a moment nothing came out. Then she gasped, covered her mouth with one hand and fell to her knees, sobbing.

"We should get back," Delilah said. "It'll be night soon."

Flossy stared at the little family again, and they stared back. She put a hand on the dome.

She accepted it now. That was her family on the other side of the dome, without her. She wished Benji would run over and put his hand against hers.

"Can't I stay?" Flossy asked. "I want to say goodbye."

"It's not safe, child," Delilah said.

"The monsters," Aylin whispered.

"That part about Rodmark *is* true," Poli added.

"I don't care," Flossy said. She didn't move. "I don't want to leave them."

The old woman sighed as Aylin and Poli walked away. "Suit yourself," Delilah said. "We'll leave a light for you outside the hovel so you can find it."

Soon Flossy was alone – with her family only metres away but impossible to reach.

"I'm sorry, Dad," Flossy muttered. "I should have listened."

As she watched them, she noticed a large shape coming up from behind the house. Was it one of the neighbours, mabye to ask about Flossy?

No, it was too large. Hulking. Monstrous.

Flossy stood up, her heart thumping in panic. Something must've slipped in through the vent before Dome Maintenance closed it. Flossy had let something horrible into Lysande, and it was about to devour her family.

Flossy pounded her fists against the dome. "Mum! Dad!" she shrieked. "You have to run! Get Benji away from here! Run!"

But the three figures turned slowly and walked back towards the house. They didn't seem to see the creature.

"Mum!" Flossy screamed again as she pounded on the dome.

Her family walked right through the beast, and that's when Flossy realized: the monster was a reflection.

She spun, and she screamed as the hulking monster fell upon her. But inside the dome no one heard her.

It was soundproof, after all.

SPACE DOMES

Why would humans want to live on other worlds? Well, because it's cool! And because scientists could better explore planets and moons if they lived on them. A dome might be the best home for those space pioneers.

A dome is the most efficient and cheapest shape for space shelters. Domes need fewer parts than traditional buildings. They can be inflated from small, light packages carried on rockets. A dome's weight is spread evenly throughout its shape, and not in just a few places. This means it could last a long time.

The domes would need to be tough, though. Earth's thick atmosphere burns up small meteors that fall to the ground. Not all planets are as lucky. A meteor the size of a tennis ball could rip through the plastic of a dome wall and let out all the oxygen!

But the hardest part of living in space could be loneliness. You couldn't drive to a friend's house. You couldn't invite Gran over for dinner — unless she rides a rocket. Being alone for a long time can even cause hallucinations. You might see strange lights or hear voices from people who aren't there ... or are they?

GLOSSARY

gust sudden, strong blast of wind

hovel small, poorly built, dirty house

irrigation method of bringing water to crops using a system of pipes or channels; also, something that helps with this process

junction place where two or more things meet

orbit travel around an object in space

protect keep safe from harm

reflection image that forms when light has bounced off a smooth, shiny object

soundproof not allowing sound to enter or leave

tamper damage or make changes that weaken something or cause it not to work well

vent opening that allows air to go out or into a closed-off space

wasteland ugly, empty land where nothing can grow or be built

ABOUT THE AUTHOR

Steve Brezenoff is the author of more than fifty chapter books for kids, including the Field Trip Mysteries series, the Ravens Pass series of thrillers and the Return to Titanic series. He's also written three young-adult novels: *Guy in Real Life*; *Brooklyn, Burning*; and *The Absolute Value of -1*. In his spare time, he enjoys video games, cycling and cooking. Steve lives in Minnesota, USA, with his wife, Beth,

ABOUT THE ILLUSTRATOR

Juan Calle is a former biologist turned science illustrator. Early on in his illustration career, he worked on field guides of plants and animals native to his country of origin, Colombia. Now he owns and works in his art studio, LIBERUM DONUM, creating concept art, storyboards and his passion: comic books.

READ MORE SCARY
SPACE ADVENTURES!

ALIEN LOCKDOWN

HAUNTED PLANET

THE FINAL MISSION

A HOLE IN THE DOME